HEIDI

By JOHANNA SPYRI · Adapted by FLORENCE HAYES

Illustrated by Erika Weihs

RANDOM HOUSE ✤ NEW YORK

ONE clear sunny morning in June two figures could be seen climbing a narrow mountain path in the Swiss Alps. One was a tall, strong-looking girl named Dete, the other a five-year-old child whom she was leading by the hand and whose little cheeks glowed bright red through her sunburnt skin.

And this was hardly to be wondered at, for in spite of the hot June sun, the child was bundled up as if to keep off the bitterest frost.

After an hour's climb they came to the hamlet of Dorfli, halfway up the mountain, which had

once been Dete's home. Heads popped out from all of the doors.

"Hello, Dete! Where are you going?" her old friends wanted to know.

Dete did not pause to reply. She held tight to the child's hand and hurried on. But when her friend Barbel called, "Wait a minute, Dete. If you're going up the mountain, I'll walk with you," Dete

stopped. The child immediately let
go her hand and sat down on the
ground.

"Are you tired, Heidi?" asked her
companion.

"No, I'm hot," answered the
child.

"We shall soon get to
the top now. You must
walk bravely on a little
longer, and take good long steps, and in another hour we shall be there," said Dete.

Now Barbel joined them and walked on ahead with Dete, while
Heidi wandered behind them.

"Where are you off to with the little girl? It's your sister's child,
isn't it?" asked Barbel.

"Yes. I'm taking her to live with her grandfather," Dete answered.

"With the Alm-Uncle? Dete!" exclaimed Barbel. "Have you lost your senses? You know what he's like. Everybody's afraid of him. He'll make you take her home again."

Dete tossed her head. "He can't do that! He's her grandfather! I've taken care of the child since her mother died, and I'm not going to give up the good position I've been offered, just for her sake. And I certainly can't take her with me."

"Why, where are you going?"

"To Frankfurt," answered Dete.

"Well, I'm glad I am not that child!" exclaimed Barbel. "The old man up there looks wild, with his bushy brows and his great beard. He never sets foot in church; and when he comes down to the village, everybody keeps out of his way."

"He's her grandfather, and he's got to take care of her," Dete insisted.

"Why does he live as he does?" asked Barbel.

"They say when he was a young man he got in with evil company and lost his farm and everything he had," Dete answered. "His parents died of grief. Then he himself disappeared and nobody heard from him until, years later, he came back with a young son, Tobias. When he found all doors closed to him, he moved to Dorfli."

"Why is he called the Alm-Uncle?" Barbel wanted to know.

"Our family called him Uncle because his son was married to my sister Adelheid, and soon the whole village called him Uncle. When Tobias was killed in an accident, leaving my sister and Heidi alone, people said it was a judgment upon the Uncle. He grew bitter and moved to the top of Alm Mountain,

vowing he would never come down. That's why people call him the Alm-Uncle."

"Well!" exclaimed Barbel when she heard this. "How you can take the child to live with him, I don't know!" At this she turned toward a little hut in a hollow and said, "I have to stop here to see about some spinning. Good luck!"

Trailing behind Dete and Barbel while they talked, Heidi had made friends with a young goatherd, Peter, who lived in a hut halfway up the Alm. Peter was eleven years old. He knew many places where there were good shrubs for his goats to nibble, and he was in the habit of leading his flock aside from the beaten path. At first Heidi had watched Peter as he sprang nimbly here and there on his bare feet, driving his goats up the steep mountain side. Then she tried to follow him.

It was hot, though, and her clothes were too heavy. All at once she sat down on the ground, and as fast as her little fingers could move, began pulling off her red, woolen scarf and her shoes and stockings. Then the dresses came off, all the dresses Dete had put on her to save the trouble of carrying them.

Now Heidi stood up, clad only in a light petticoat, and stretched out her little bare arms with glee. She put all her clothes together in a tidy heap, and went jumping and climbing after Peter and the goats.

Dete was very cross when she saw what Heidi had done, and scolded her. She made Peter go back and pick up the clothes and carry them the rest of the way.

At the end of another hour's climb, Heidi and Dete and Peter reached the Alm-Uncle's hut on the top of the mountain. On a bench before the hut sat the old man, smoking his pipe and looking over the valley below. Heidi went straight to him and said, "Good evening, Grandfather!"

"What's the meaning of this?" he asked gruffly.

"Good evening, Uncle," said Dete, stepping forward. "I've brought Tobias' little girl to you. I've done my duty by her. Now you must do yours."

"So!" said the old man. "What can a child do with me up here? What if she begins to fret for you?"

"That's your affair," retorted Dete. "If harm comes to her, you will be answerable."

At that the old man rose, his eyes flashing. "Be off with you," he thundered, "and do not let me see your face again in a hurry."

"Good-bye, then," said Dete quickly. "And good-bye to you, too, Heidi." And she turned and almost ran down the mountain.

WHILE the Alm-Uncle sat down to think, Heidi ran off to investigate her new surroundings. She peeped into the shed where the goats were kept. She went behind the hut to the tall fir trees and listened to the wind blowing through their branches. When she came back, her grandfather was still sitting on his bench, puffing away at his pipe. She walked up to him.

"What is it you want?" he asked.

"I want to see what you have inside the house," answered Heidi.

"Bring your bundle of clothes in with you," he said, rising and opening the door.

"I shan't want them any more," was her prompt answer.

The old man turned and looked at her. "And why shall you not want them any more?" he asked.

"Because I want to go about like the goats with their thin light legs."

"Well, you can do so if you like," said her grandfather, "but bring the things in, we must put them in the cupboard."

The hut had
only one large room.
Heidi took it in at a glance: the table,
the chair, the old man's bed, the kettle
hanging over the fireplace. A door in the wall
opened onto a cupboard.

On one shelf were dishes; on another, bread, cheese, and dried
meat; on the third, the Uncle's clothes. Heidi pushed her bundle to
the back of this shelf.

She looked carefully round the room and asked, "Where am I to sleep, Grandfather?"

"Wherever you like," he answered.

She saw a ladder that reached to the floor above, and quickly climbed up. There was a hayloft with a large round window overlooking the valley. "Oh, it's lovely! I shall sleep up here, Grandfather," she called down, "but I'll need a sheet," and she began to gather the sweet-scented hay.

Together they arranged a bed, with hay for a mattress and two thick sacks for a sheet and a cover. "I wish it were night so I could get into this lovely bed now," Heidi said.

"Hadn't we better eat first?" Grandfather asked.

Heidi followed him down the ladder and watched him go to the hearth and swing the kettle over the fire. Then he put some cheese on a long fork and held it

over the flame, turning it until it was toasted a nice golden yellow. Heidi set the table.

"What will you do for a seat?" Grandfather asked.

Heidi ran to the hearth and fetched a small three-legged stool. But it was so low she could not reach the table. Grandfather filled a bowl with warm milk, set it on the chair, and drew it up before Heidi where she sat on her low stool. Then he laid the toasted cheese on some bread and told her to eat. After

which he sat down on the corner of the table and began his own meal.

Heidi soon emptied her bowl. "It's the best milk I ever drank," she said. Grandfather filled her bowl again. When they had finished eating, Heidi followed him out to a shed where he began working with his tools. Soon she saw he had made a three-legged stool like his, only with longer legs. "It's for me, I know," she said, delighted to have something of her own.

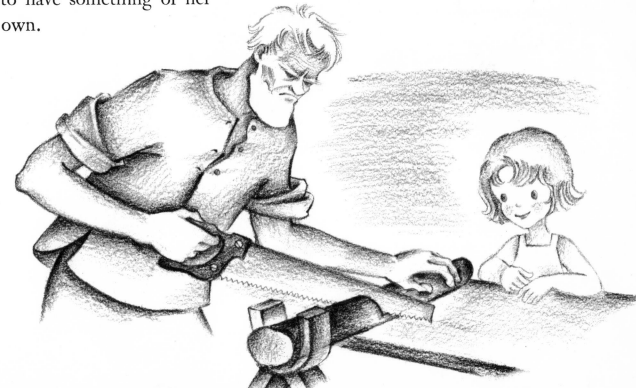

Evening came, and the wind sang through the fir trees louder than ever. Soon Heidi heard a shrill whistle, and down from the heights came Peter and his goats. Heidi ran outside to see two of them come up to her grandfather and lick the salt he held in his hands, as Peter and the others disappeared down the mountain side.

"Are these two ours?" Heidi asked excitedly.

"Yes," said Grandfather, "their names are White Swan and Little Bear. Go get your bowl and some bread." And when he had milked White Swan he filled the bowl, and told Heidi to eat and run off to bed.

"Good night, Grandfather," Heidi called, as he took his goats to the shed. A few minutes later she climbed the ladder and hurried into her bed.

Before you could spell her name, she was sleeping as happily as a princess on a silken couch.

The next morning a loud whistle woke Heidi. Hearing her grandfather's voice, she jumped up, dressed, and hurried down the ladder.

There stood Peter with his goats, waiting for the Uncle to bring his to join them.

"Do you want to go up the mountain with Peter?" asked Grandfather. Heidi was delighted. "Then wash and tidy yourself," he said, "or the sun will laugh at you." He put a large piece of bread and cheese for Heidi into Peter's lunch box, handed him a bowl and

said, "Milk two bowlfuls for her at noon. And take care she does not fall over the rocks."

As they started up the mountain, Heidi dashed this way and that to look at the beautiful flowers. Sometimes she would run ahead and sit down in a field of blossoms and Peter would have to call to know where she was. "She's as bad as the goats," he grumbled. "Now I must watch them and her too."

When they came to the place where he usually halted his goats to pasture, Peter laid his lunch box in a hollow so the wind wouldn't blow it away, and threw himself down for a nap. Heidi filled her apron with flowers, then sat down beside. him. How beautiful was

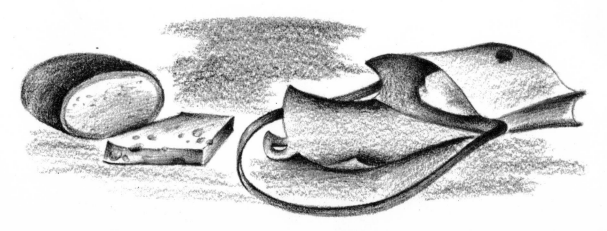

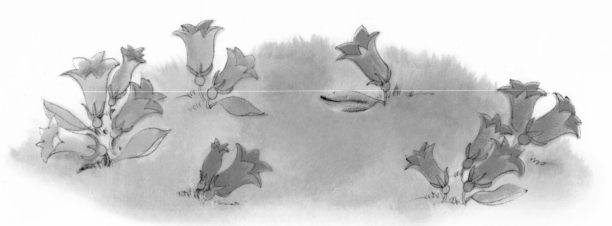

the snow on the peaks! How beautiful the green valley! And she had never seen so many flowers in her life!

Peter's stomach soon told him it was time to eat, so he sat up and opened his lunch box. He laid Heidi's bread and cheese to one side, and his to the other. Then he filled the bowl with White Swan's milk and called Heidi. She drank two bowls of milk, but she broke off only a small piece of bread.

The rest and the cheese she handed to Peter, saying, "You may have it." He thought at first she must be joking. When he saw that she meant it, he set to on the biggest lunch he had had in a long time.

Much later Heidi saw that the sun was casting a reddish glow over the peaks, the snow, and the flowers. "Peter!

Isn't it beautiful!" she cried. But Peter had no eye for sunsets. He had seen too many.

"It's time to go," he said.

Just then he caught sight of one of the goats taking leaps in the direction of the cliff, and, dashing up to it, lifted his stick to give it a good beating as punishment.

Heidi cried out. "You have no right to touch her, it will hurt her. Let her alone!"

"I'll let her off if you will give me some more of your cheese tomorrow," said Peter.

"You shall have it all, tomorrow and every day; but you must promise never to beat any of the goats," Heidi said.

"All right," Peter promised. "I don't care."

Day after day Heidi went up the mountain with Peter and his herd. She grew healthy and brown in the sun, and as carefree as the birds.

They shot down the mountain so fast that Heidi thought they were flying.

When they reached Peter's hut, Grand-father said, "As soon as it begins

to grow dark, you must come home." And he went back up the mountain.

In the hut, Peter's mother was mending his coat; the old grand-mother sat in the corner, spinning.

Heidi walked up to her and said, "Good morning, Grandmother. I've come at last."

"It's the child who lives with the Alm-Uncle, isn't it?" the grand-

At last fall came, and with it, heavier and stronger winds. Often Grandfather would say, "You must stay at home today, Heidi, or the wind will blow you over the rocks."

Peter did not like this. He hated to miss that extra lunch. Besides, the goats had grown so used to Heidi that they would refuse to go unless she was with them. But she did not mind staying at home. She liked following Grandfather about, watching him making cheese, or working with his tools.

Finally it grew so cold that she had to put on the shoes and stockings she had hidden in the cupboard. Then one morning a blanket of snow lay over the mountain.

Now Peter and his goats stopped coming altogether, for there was not a green thing to be seen. It snowed until Heidi thought the hut would be buried in it. Then one day it stopped, and Grandfather went out to shovel paths.

That afternoon there came a thump at the door, and in walked Peter. The Alm-Uncle invited him to stay for supper.

How Peter's eyes popped when the old man handed him some bread with a big piece of meat on it!

When he had finished eating, Peter said, "I must go now. Grandmother sent word that she would like Heidi to come and see her one day."

Almost as soon as Heidi was up the next morning, she announced, "I must go to see Peter's grandmother today. She will be expecting me."

Grandfather told her to wait until the snow was not so deep. But each day she said the same thing. On the fourth morning the snow was hard as ice.

"All right then," Grandfather said this time. "Come along."

He wrapped Heidi in the heavy sack from her bed, and dragged the sled out of the shed. Then he sat on the low seat, took Heidi on his lap, and pushed off with his foot.

mother asked, pleased that she had come. As they talked, one of the shutters flapped against the window.

"See that! It will break the window," Heidi said. "Grandfather must fix it."

The grandmother said she could hear it slap and feel the old house shake, but she could not see anything, for she was blind. That made Heidi very sad. "Who can make it light for you again? Can no one do it?" she cried. It took the grandmother a long time to quiet her.

Heidi stayed at the hut until Peter came home from school.
"How is the reading getting on?" asked the grandmother.
"Not very well," was Peter's answer.

The old woman sighed. "Ah well," she said, "I hoped you would have something different to tell me. Up there on the shelf is an old prayer book, with beautiful songs in it which I have not heard for a long time. I hoped that you would soon learn enough to be able to read one of them to me sometimes."

When it grew dark, Heidi said, "I must go now, but I'll come to-morrow."

Grandfather met her outside, wrapped the sack around her, and carried her up the mountain.

Heidi told him about the flapping shutter and the shaky house. "We must go tomorrow with the hammer and fix it," she said.

"Who says so?" Grandfather wanted to know.

Heidi told him that nobody had said so. She knew it herself. "The grandmother lies awake when the wind blows because she is afraid the house will fall down. She is blind, too. You could help her, couldn't you?"

"At least we can fix the rattling," Grandfather said.

And the next day when he and Heidi went down to the hut, he took along his hammer and nails. In fact, every time he went down he took his tools along and spent many hours making the cottage sound and tight. He would never go in-side, though, even to be thanked for his work, for he did not believe people ever meant to be kind. When he was finished, the hut no longer groaned and rattled the whole night through, and the grandmother said she would never forget what the Alm-Uncle had done for her.

THE winter passed, summer had gone its way, and now another winter was almost over. Heidi was nearly eight, yet she had never been to school. The teacher at Dorfli sent word by Peter that she must come to school at once. Grandfather sent word back that she was not coming, now or ever. Then the pastor from the village came up to see the Alm-Uncle. He, too, said that Heidi must go to school and that the Alm-Uncle should move to the village so she need not miss a day. Grandfather shook his head. "The people of Dorfli despise me, and I them. It's better we live apart."

"My friend, if you will make your peace with God, you will see how quickly people will be friendly," the pastor replied. But the Alm-Uncle said he would never move to the village. And for the next few days, he did not even take Heidi down to see Peter's grandmother.

Then suddenly one afternoon, Dete walked into the hut, in a feathered hat and a long trailing dress. She praised Heidi's appearance, saying, "I can see she's had good care, Uncle, but I know she must be in your way so I've come to take her with me." The Alm-Uncle just stared at her. "Some wealthy relatives of the people I serve are looking for a companion for their young invalid daughter," she went on. "No one can say what might happen. They might even adopt——"

"Have you finished?" snapped the old man.

Dete was angry. "I'm responsible for my sister's child," she retorted, "and she must go to school. Everybody in Dorfli agrees with me. I advise you to think it over before letting the matter go to court."

The Alm-Uncle's eyes flashed. "Be gone, with your hat and feathers, and such words on your tongue," he shouted, and strode out of the hut.

Dete told Heidi to get her clothes quickly.

"But I'm not going to leave Grandfather," said the little girl.

"Nonsense!" said Dete. "In Frankfurt you will have all sorts of nice things."

When Heidi did not move, Dete found her clothes, and, taking the girl by the hand, almost dragged her down the mountain. "If you don't like it, you can come back whenever you wish," she said as Heidi began to cry.

When they reached the grandmother's hut, Heidi wanted to stop to say good-bye, but Dete would not let her. "You can bring her something nice when you come home, maybe some soft white rolls. She's too old to eat hard bread."

Pleased at the thought of doing something for the grandmother, Heidi said no more and went with Dete.

It was the evening of the next day when Heidi and Dete reached the home of Herr Sesemann in Frankfurt and were shown to the study where Clara, the invalid daughter, lay waiting on her couch. At a small table, embroidering, sat Fraulein Rottenmeier, the housekeeper, with a queer-looking cap on her head. Fraulein looked Heidi over, and did not seem pleased with her appearance.

"Can you read?" she asked. Heidi said that she could not. Fraulein was shocked. "How old are you?" she went on. Dete answered quickly that she must be about ten. Heidi said she was eight.

"Eight!" exclaimed Fraulein. "You know Clara is twelve. I asked for a companion her own age. This child cannot even read. How could you think of bringing her to me!"

"I thought she seemed made for the place," said Dete. Then, fearing there was to be trouble, she added, "I must be going now. My mistress expects me," and backed out of the room before

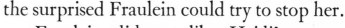

the surprised Fraulein could try to stop her. Fraulein did not like Heidi's name, either, and declared, "You were baptized Adelheid and that is what I shall call you."

But Clara smiled, and said, "If your name is Heidi, I will call you Heidi." She said it would be fun to have her as a companion, and was sure she would soon learn to read under her kind tutor.

In spite of her unhappiness, the first thing Heidi noticed as she sat at the big table at dinner that evening, was a soft white roll by her plate. She asked Sebastian, the butler, if she might have it, and when he

nodded his head she tucked it into her pocket to take to the grandmother.

Fraulein said, with a sigh: "I see I shall have to teach you some table manners," and she went on with a long list. But Clara laughed and said that the little girl had not heard a word. She was so tired from her long journey that she had fallen fast asleep!

THE next morning when Heidi awoke she wondered where she was. Then she remembered the big house Dete had brought her to, and jumping out of bed, ran from window to window trying to see grass and mountains. She saw nothing but walls. It was as though she were shut in a cage. She was dressing to run outdoors, as she did at home, when the maid Tinette knocked and said breakfast was ready. And as soon as she and Clara finished eating, they went straight to the study to wait for the tutor. Clara told Heidi how kind he was, and Heidi told Clara about her grandfather and his hut and Peter.

The moment the tutor arrived, Fraulein took him aside and told him that Heidi could not read. She hoped he would say that she must be sent home. But instead he said patience was all that was needed. That did not please Fraulein, but she did not dare send the little girl away of her own accord.

And so Heidi began her schooling. An hour later Fraulein heard the sound of a frightful crash in the study. She rushed into the room. On the floor lay books, inkstand, and other articles, while from beneath them a dark stream of ink was flowing all across the floor. Heidi was nowhere to be seen. She had disappeared.

Fraulein ran down the stairs. There, at the bottom, standing in the open doorway, was Heidi, looking in amazement up and down the street.

"What are you doing? What are you thinking of to run away like that?" cried Fraulein.

"I heard the sound of fir trees, but I can't see where they are, and now I can't hear them any more," answered Heidi.

"Fir trees!" repeated Fraulein scornfully. "Do you suppose we are in a wood? What a silly idea! The sound you heard came from the passing carriages. Come upstairs and see the mischief you have done!" Heidi followed Fraulein Rottenmeier upstairs; she was quite surprised when she saw the damage, for in her hurry she had not realized what she was doing.

"I'll excuse you this time, but don't let it happen again," said Fraulein, pointing to the floor. "During your lesson time you are to sit still and pay attention. If you don't, I shall have to tie you to the chair. Do you understand?"

"Yes," replied Heidi. She had learned another rule.

But for some reason, for all the tutor's patience, Heidi did not learn easily. She grew more and more unhappy, and whenever she talked with Clara, she would say, "Tomorrow I must go home to Grandfather." Clara said she must wait until Herr Sesemann came home. So each day Heidi put two more rolls in her closet to take to the old blind grandmother.

In the afternoons, when Clara was resting, Heidi was left to amuse herself. One day she slipped out into the street and, with the kindly assistance of an organ grinder, set off in the direction of a tower with a golden dome which she had often seen from her window. It was a church. Heidi went in. When she came out, she was carrying a little kitten in each of her pockets! The tower-keeper, whose cat had just had a new litter of kittens, had given them to her. Heidi was late for dinner that night; the others were already seated at the table.

Fraulein was very cross. "You behaved very badly," she scolded, "running out of the house as you did, without asking permission, without anyone's know-

ing where you went, and then coming back here at such an hour."

"Miau!" came the answer.

Fraulein became very angry. "How dare you make a joke of it!"

"I did not"—began Heidi—"Miau, miau!"

"That will do," said Fraulein. "Get up and leave the room!"

"But Heidi," put in Clara, "when you see that it makes Fraulein angry, why do you keep on saying 'miau'?"

"It's not I, it's the kittens in my pocket," Heidi was at last given time to say.

"Kittens!" shrieked Fraulein. "Take them away!"

And she rushed out of the room, while Heidi and Clara quickly arranged with Sebastian to hide the kittens in a place where Fraulein was not likely to find them.

Often, when she was not playing with the kittens, Heidi would sit in her room by herself, thinking of the time when she would return to her mountains. One day she felt she could stand it no longer. She must run away. She wrapped all the rolls in her red shawl, put on her old straw hat, and got as far as the front door, when Fraulein caught her. How she scolded! Heidi cried and said that she just had to go home. But Fraulein called Sebastian, and Heidi went back to her room. That night, as usual, she put a roll in her pocket. But she did not touch her dinner.

A few days later Fraulein went through Heidi's clothes closet to see what she would need before Herr Sesemann came home, and she discovered the rolls! "Tinette! Throw this stale bread away. And that old straw hat, too!" she ordered.

"No!" screamed Heidi, trying to stop her.

"I must keep the hat, and the rolls are for the grandmother." But Fraulein pulled her away and Tinette went off with the things. Heidi threw herself onto Clara's couch and wept.

"Don't cry," Clara said, trying to comfort her. "You'll have fresh rolls to take to the grandmother when you go."

Heidi dried her tears. That night when she went to bed, she found her old straw hat where Sebastian had hidden it under her bedspread. Happily she hid it in a corner of her closet.

Then one day there was much excitement in the house. Herr Sesemann, Clara's father, had come home, and everyone was bustling about, carrying boxes from his carriage. But no sooner had he entered the house than Fraulein began to tell him about Heidi and how unfit she was to be a companion for Clara. Herr Sesemann listened, asked questions, and said he would see what Clara had to say. Of course, Clara wanted Heidi to stay. That was all Herr Sesemann needed to know. If Clara liked her, she must stay. Fraulein was not pleased at his decision. But Herr Sesemann told her that if she could not manage, she must remember that his mother was coming soon, and *she* could get along with anybody!

In a few days Herr Sesemann returned to Paris. Soon a letter came

from his mother, telling just when she would arrive. There was so much talk about "Grandmamma," as Clara called her, that Heidi began calling her Grandmamma, too. At this Fraulein frowned and said, "Remember, you are always to address Frau Sesemann as 'Madam!' Do you understand?" Heidi did not, but would ask no questions.

She liked Clara's grandmamma the moment she saw her. She liked her kind voice and her beautiful white hair. But when Heidi called her "Madam" Grandmamma laughed and said, "You may call me Grandmamma, as Clara does."

That afternoon while Clara was resting, Grandmamma looked for Heidi. She was shocked to find that the little girl was alone in her room. "Bring her to me at once," she said to Fraulein. "I have some books for her."

"Oh, she doesn't read!" said Fraulein. "She can't even learn her ABC's."

"That's strange! She doesn't look to me like a stupid child," said Grandmamma. "Well, she can look at the pictures."

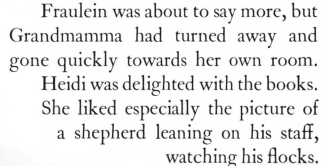

Fraulein was about to say more, but Grandmamma had turned away and gone quickly towards her own room. Heidi was delighted with the books. She liked especially the picture of a shepherd leaning on his staff, watching his flocks.

But as she looked at it, she burst into tears.

"Don't cry, dear child. The picture has reminded you of something," Grandmamma said kindly. But for a long time Heidi could not control her tears. When she was quiet again, Grandmamma said, "How are you getting along with your lessons? Have you learned to read?"

"No," answered Heidi. "But I knew before I started that it was impossible. Peter told me so. He tried and couldn't learn."

"How odd Peter must be!" Grandmamma said. "Of course you can learn. And when you can read the story that goes with that picture, I will give you the book." She gave Heidi her first lesson that day.

Grandmamma knew that the little girl was unhappy, but she did not know why. Heidi would not tell her for fear she and Clara would think her ungrateful for their kindness. Grandmamma told her that she must tell God about it in her prayers. He would surely help her.

A sudden gleam of joy came into Heidi's eyes. "May I tell Him everything, everything?"

"Yes, Heidi, everything," Grandmamma said.

Heidi drew away her hand, which Grandmamma had been holding affectionately between her own, and said, "May I go?"

"Yes, of course," was the answer, and Heidi ran off at once to her own room and, kneeling on the floor, told God that she wanted to return to her grandfather.

One morning, a week or so later, the tutor asked if he might speak to Frau Sesemann.

"I have surprising news," he said. "Heidi can read!"

But if the tutor was surprised, Grandmamma was not. She had found that Heidi

learned easily. But she went down to the study to see for herself. There sat Heidi, reading aloud to Clara! That evening at dinner Heidi found the book at her plate.

Nothing pleased the little girl more than to be asked to read aloud. But the story that she liked best always made her the saddest —the story of the shepherd Joseph. "The Prodigal Son," Grand-

mamma called it. One picture showed him at home tending the sheep; the next, in a strange land, lonely and forsaken; the third, returning to his native land, ragged but happy to be back home again. Heidi never tired of hearing Grandmamma tell this story.

Every day she learned something new—to sew and make dolls' clothes, to read ever so many new stories. Still Grandmamma knew that she was not happy. One day she asked, "Have you told God about the thing that makes you unhappy?" Heidi said she had. "And do you still pray to Him?" Heidi said she did not. Grandmamma asked why.

"It's no use," sighed Heidi. "For weeks I've prayed for the same thing, and He does not give it to me. But I can understand that. There must be hundreds in Frankfurt asking for things."

"You must not stop praying," Grandmamma said. "God will think you have forsaken Him."

Heidi went at once to ask God to forgive her and promised she would not forget Him again.

Soon it was time for Grandmamma to be returning home. And when she left, how big and silent the house seemed! One afternoon Heidi was reading aloud to Clara to pass the time when she happened upon a story about a grandmother dying.

"Oh!" she cried out, "then the grandmother is dead!" and burst into tears.

Clara explained that it was only a story and had nothing to do with the grandmother on the mountain. But Heidi, now more homesick than ever, felt that she would never see her friends again. When Fraulein heard her crying, she came and scolded her, saying: "Now, that's enough of all this nonsense. If you start crying again while you are reading, I shall take the book away from you and shall not let you have it again." Heidi at once dried her tears. She could not bear to lose her dearest possession. But though

she never cried again when she read, it did not mean that she was less homesick. She grew pale and lost her appetite and became so thin that Sebastian noticed it and tried his hardest to make her eat.

But it was of no use. Heidi scarcely ate anything at all, and when she went to bed at night she buried her face in her pillow and wept.

Weeks passed. At last autumn came, then the winter, then another spring. It made no difference to Heidi. The walls and windows she looked upon showed no change, and she never went out-of-doors except when Clara was well enough to be taken for a drive.

Even then they went only a little way, and though they saw fine streets and large houses and crowds of people, they never saw grass and flowers or fir trees and mountains.

It was these things that Heidi longed for more and more.

In her lonely room she would think of Grandfather's hut, of the grandmother, of Peter and the goats, the golden flowers in the sunlight, and the bright colors of the rocks at sunset.

And each time she thought of them she grew a little sadder. They seemed so far away.

FOR days there had been mysterious happenings in the Sesemann household. No matter how fast the door was barred at night, when the servants went downstairs in the morning it was always open. It could not be a thief; nothing was ever missing. Could it be a ghost? This thought made Fraulein so nervous that she would not go into any of the empty rooms without Tinette. Tinette would not go upstairs or down unless Sebastian went along. Sebastian never peeped into a dark corner unless John the footman were at his heels, nor would John go anywhere without Sebastian.

All day long the cook would say, "That I should live to hear of such a thing!" Of course no one spoke of these things before the children.

Fraulein finally persuaded Sebastian and John to sit up all night and find out who was doing the mischief. One evening they armed themselves with several weapons and took up their watch. They ate and talked and dozed. Around midnight Sebastian tried to rouse John, but could not. Then at one o'clock John sat up and said, as though he were a man of courage, "Come, Sebastian. We must see what's going on."

But as he stepped into the hall a gust of wind blew out the candle, and he fell back against Sebastian, nearly upsetting him.

When Sebastian lighted the candle again, John was as white as a ghost.

"What did you see?" Sebastian asked.

"It's open," gasped John, "and there's a white figure on the stairs."

Shivering, they sat down and did not stir from their seats until daybreak. Then they went out and closed and barred the door, and hastened to tell Fraulein of their experience.

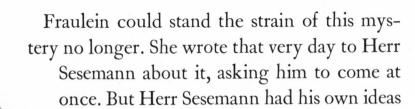

Fraulein could stand the strain of this mystery no longer. She wrote that very day to Herr Sesemann about it, asking him to come at once. But Herr Sesemann had his own ideas about ghosts. "You and the servants should be able to solve this mystery," he replied. "If not, write for my my mother to come. *She* is not afraid of anything." So Fraulein wrote to Frau Sesemann. Frau Sesemann answered that she had no intention of returning to look for a ghost. "If there's one in the house, it must be alive, and you ought to be able to deal with it, Rottenmeier," she wrote.

Now Fraulein was angry. Herr Sesemann must come home, and she knew a way to bring him. She wrote him that the ghost was making Clara more and more nervous and that she might become very ill unless something were done about it.

He came on the next train.

Herr Sesemann suspected Sebastian of playing tricks on Fraulein and began at once to question him. But he soon saw that Sebastian was as frightened as Fraulein.

So he sent for his friend, the doctor who attended Clara, and that night they took up their watch in the same room in which Sebastian and John had waited.

They lighted a candle and laid their loaded revolvers between them.

Then they talked and waited until the clock struck twelve.

Then one.

And then—they heard the bar of the outer door being lifted!

"Who's there?" roared the doctor, opening the door.

A little white figure turned. It was Heidi —barefooted and shivering.

"What are you doing here, child?" asked the kindly doctor.

Heidi did not know. The doctor lifted her in his arms, carried her upstairs, and put her in her bed. When she stopped trembling, he asked if she had been dreaming.

"Yes," she said, "I dream every night of being at home with Grandfather. But when I wake in the morning, I am always in my bed in Frankfurt."

When the doctor heard this, he said, "Go to sleep now, Heidi. Everything will be all right tomorrow."

He went downstairs and told Herr Sesemann, "She must go

back at once to her mountains. She's sick and thin as a skeleton."
Herr Sesemann was shocked that this should have happened in his
house without anyone's noticing it. "But first we must make her
sound and strong," he protested.

"Her illness cannot be cured by pills," the doctor said, adding
that if she were sent home at once, she might recover in the mountain air. Herr Sesemann understood and agreed.

At daybreak he went upstairs and awakened Fraulein and the
servants. "Come down at once," he ordered. "We must prepare for
a journey."

Frightened, they jumped out of their beds. Had the ghost at-
tacked the master, and were they being called to his assistance? With
pale faces, they crept into the dining room. John
was sent for the carriage; Sebastian to bring
Dete to the house; Tinette to wake Heidi and
dress her. Just then Fraulein came into the
room, so befuddled that she had
put her cap on backwards. Herr
Sesemann told her to get
out a trunk and pack all
Heidi's things in it and a
good part of Clara's, too.
Meanwhile he would go up
to wake his daughter and
break the news to her.

Clara was distressed at losing her companion, but when her father explained that Heidi was homesick, she understood. "Just let Heidi's trunk be brought in here so that I may put in some things for her," she said.

Sebastian returned with Dete at his heels in a great state of excitement. Why was Heidi being sent home? As for herself, she was sorry, but she could not get away just now. Her mistress needed her. She was thinking of Uncle's last words to her, and did not want to see him again.

So Sebastian was put in charge of the little girl on her journey. "When you stop at the hotel tonight," Herr Sesemann warned him, "be sure her windows are fastened, so that they cannot be easily opened. After Heidi is in bed, lock the door of her room on the outside, for she walks in her sleep and might hurt herself if she went wandering·downstairs and tried to open the front door. Do you understand?"

"So that was it!" Sebastian exclaimed, remembering the open door.

"Yes," said Herr Sesemann, "and you are all idiots for not finding it out for yourselves."

And with that Herr Sesemann went off to his study to write a letter to the Alm-Uncle.

Perhaps Heidi was the most surprised of all at being called so early in the morning. Tinette put on her best dress without telling her why. When Herr Sesemann explained that she was going back to her grandfather, she was too excited to eat. She ran up to Clara's room to wait for the carriage.

"See what I have put in the trunk for you!" cried Clara, pointing to it in the middle of the room. Then she showed her dresses and aprons and handkerchiefs, and other lovely things. "And

look here," she added, as she held up a basket. Inside were twelve soft, white rolls for the grandmother.

Heidi had never been happier.

Someone announced that the carriage was ready, and Heidi ran to her room to get her book from under her pillow. Then she took her shawl from the closet, put her old hat in it, and placed the two on top of her basket. Fraulein tried to take the shawl from her, but Herr Sesemann said she might keep it.

Soon Heidi was on her way to the train, the basket of rolls on her knees. "Are you sure the grandmother is not dead?" she kept asking Sebastian.

"I don't see why she should be," he would answer. And Heidi would be comforted for a while.

When they reached Mayenfeld, Sebastian found a man with a cart who agreed to take Heidi to Dorfli. "I can go by myself from there," Heidi said. Sebastian paid the man well for his trouble, then handed the little girl a package for herself and a letter for her grandfather from Herr Sesemann, and told her to take good care not to lose them. She put them in her basket under the rolls.

THE peaks looked down on Heidi like old friends, and the trees seemed to wave a welcome home. She thought the cart would never reach Dorfli. But at last it stopped and she jumped out, still holding her basket.

"Thank you," she said to the man. "Grandfather will come for the trunk tomorrow."

Would she find the grandmother by the spinning wheel? She kept asking herself that question as she hurried up the steep path. At last she saw the little hut in the hollow, and ran in, calling, "Grandmother! Grandmother! I'm back."

The grandmother was too surprised to speak. But when she put her hand on Heidi's hair, she said, "It is indeed the little girl. God has granted my prayer."

Heidi laid the rolls in the old woman's lap. "There, Grandmother!" she said. "Now you won't have to eat hard bread for days."

Peter's mother was as surprised and happy as the grandmother was to see Heidi. "What a pretty hat you have on!" she said.

"You shall have it, for I do not need it any more," said Heidi. She put on the old hat that she had worn when she went away. She remembered what Grandfather had said about Dete and her feathers!

Then she took off her pretty dress and put on her old shawl.

"I want Grandfather to see me as I used to be so he will surely know me," she said, and hurried up the mountain.

How good it was to be home again! Everything was even more beautiful than she had remembered it. At last she saw the tops of the

fir trees, then the roof of her grandfather's hut, then the whole of it. There,
before it, as in the old days, sat Grandfather puffing away at his pipe.
Heidi dropped her basket and rushed to him, flinging her arms
round his neck.

"Grandfather! Grandfather!" was all she could say.

The old man took Heidi on his knees and looked at her. "Did they send you away?" he asked.

"Oh, no, Grandfather. They were very kind. I just wanted to come back to you. I think it's all in the letter," she said, handing it and the package to him. But he gave the package back, saying "That's yours." The letter he read and put in his pocket.

"Now you must have some milk," Grandfather said, rising to go inside. "Bring the package with you. There is money in it for you. You can buy a nice bed and bedclothes and dresses for a couple of years with it."

"I don't want the money. I have a bed and Clara gave me plenty of dresses," Heidi said.

"Take it and put it in the cupboard; you will want it some day, I have no doubt."

Heidi obeyed and skipped happily after her grandfather into the house; she looked into every corner of the room, then she ran up the ladder to the loft above. "Oh Grandfather! My bed's gone," she said. Grandfather said they would make another.

Later, as they sat at the table eating, Heidi said, "Grandfather, this is the best milk in the world." The old man smiled.

"So you're back again!" exclaimed Peter when he came with the goats. "Will you go up the mountain tomorrow?"

"Not tomorrow, but the day after, perhaps," said Heidi, "for tomorrow I must go down to see the grandmother."

That night Grandfather went up the ladder a dozen times to

make sure Heidi was not going to walk in her sleep, as Herr Sesemann wrote she had done in Frankfurt. But Heidi was resting well. She was in her own mountains again with her grandfather, happier than she had been since she left.

The next morning Grandfather went to Dorfli for the trunk, while Heidi stopped at Peter's hut to see how the grandmother liked her rolls.

"I believe they have made me stronger already," the old woman told her, with a grateful smile.

"I shall write Clara to send you more when these are gone," Heidi promised. Then she thought of the money Herr Sesemann had given her.

She would use that to buy more rolls!

"No, no, I cannot let you. It's your money," the grandmother said; but Heidi was determined. She was sure if the grandmother grew strong she would be able to see again.

"Shall I read you one of the hymns from your book?" Heidi asked a moment later.

The grandmother could hardly believe a child so young could read when Peter did not know one word from another.

But Heidi got the book off the shelf and read until the old woman's face was

alight with joy. Then Grandfather knocked at the window. Heidi left, promising to come back the next day.

When she told her grandfather that she wanted to use her money to buy rolls for the grandmother, he asked, "But what about your bed? It would be nice to have a proper bed." Heidi replied that she slept better on hay than on her fine bed in Frankfurt. "The money is yours. Do what you like with it," he agreed then.

For a while they walked along in silence. Suddenly Heidi said, "Everything has turned out as Grandmamma said it would. If I had come home when I wanted to, the grandmother would have had only a few rolls, and I would not have been able to read to her. I'm glad God did not let me have what I asked for at once. Now I shall always pray to God, and when He does not do anything I ask for I shall think to myself, 'Perhaps He is going to do something better still.' We will pray every day now, won't we, and never forget Him again."

"What if one has forgotten God?" asked Grandfather.

"Then everything goes wrong. Grandmamma told me so," Heidi answered. "And people say you ran away from God, when He would have helped you if you had let Him."

"But if we have forgotten God, we cannot go back," Grandfather murmured.

"Oh, yes we can. There's a story in my book that explains it." When they reached home she got down her book and read the story aloud. It was of the prodigal son, who when he had wasted his life and money, went back to his father and was forgiven. "You see?" said Heidi. "We can go back."

That night as she lay asleep, Grandfather stood looking at her a long time. Then he prayed, "Father, I have sinned against God and man. I am not worthy to be called Thy son."

Early the next morning Grandfather called up to Heidi, "Put on your best dress and come down. We're going to church."

She was too surprised to ask any questions.

But it did not take her long to get ready.

When she came down the ladder, there stood Grandfather in a coat with shining silver buttons. "Grandfather!" she cried. "I've never seen you look so nice."

As they walked down the mountain the church bells rang out from the valley below, and the nearer

they walked, the
sweeter was the music. By
the time they reached the
church, the congregation had gath-
ered and was singing. Women turned to
look and lost their places in their books. "See
that!" they whispered. "The Alm-Uncle has come to
church!" The pastor was happy indeed.

When the services were over, Grandfather took Heidi to the
pastor's home. Then how the people talked! "Maybe he's not so bad
after all!" some said. "See how he takes the little one by the hand!"

The Alm-Uncle announced he was going to follow the pastor's
advice and move to Dorfli the next winter so that Heidi could go to
school. The pastor was pleased, and shook his hand warmly. Now the
congregation, too, went up to shake hands, each trying to be first.
And when the Alm-Uncle told them he was going to move to Dorfli
for the winter, they walked halfway up the mountain with him.

"Grandfather, you just look nicer and nicer today," Heidi said
when they were alone.

He smiled. "It is good to be at peace with God and man," he said. "God was good when He sent you to my hut." This time when they reached Peter's house, the two walked in together. "Good morning, Grandmother!" said Uncle.

"That I should live to see such a thing!" exclaimed the surprised old woman. "May God reward you for all you have done for me. And if I have ever injured you, do not punish me by sending the child away again while I live."

"Have no fear," said Uncle.

Just then Peter rushed in with a letter for Heidi, the first she had ever had. It was from Clara. She told her how they missed her in Frankfurt, and promised that next summer she and Grandmamma would come to visit her. "Grandmamma," she wrote, "is sending some coffee to go with the grandmother's rolls."

There was such excitement at all this news that no one noticed how the time was passing, until Uncle reminded Heidi they must be going home. "Come again soon," the grandmother said. And Uncle promised they would, the very next day. As he and Heidi climbed up the mountain toward home, the evening chimes rang out like a lovely song. Heidi was happier than she had been in all her life. And so, I think, was her grandfather.

RANDOM HOUSE BOOKS FOR CHILDREN

Question and Answer Books

For ages 6-10:
Question and Answer Book of Nature
Question and Answer Book of Science
Question and Answer Book of Space
Question and Answer Book About the
Human Body

Gateway Books

For ages 8 and up:
The Friendly Dolphins
The Horse that Swam Away
Champ: Gallant Collie
Mystery of the Musical Umbrella
and other titles

Step-Up Books

For ages 7-8:
Animals Do the Strangest Things
Birds Do the Strangest Things
Fish Do the Strangest Things
Meet Abraham Lincoln
Meet John F. Kennedy
and other titles

Babar Books

For ages 4 and up:
The Story of Babar
Babar the King
The Travels of Babar
Babar Comes to America
and other titles

Books by Dr. Seuss

For ages 5 and up:
Dr. Seuss's Sleep Book
Happy Birthday to You!
Horton Hatches the Egg
Horton Hears a Who
If I Ran the Zoo
I Had Trouble in Getting to Solla
Sollew
McElligot's Pool
On Beyond Zebra
Scrambled Eggs Super!
The Sneetches
Thidwick: The Big-Hearted Moose
Yertle the Turtle
and other titles

Giant Picture Books

For ages 5 and up:
Abraham Lincoln
Big Black Horse
Big Book of Things to Do and
Make
Big Book of Tricks and Magic
Blue Fairy Book
Daniel Boone
Famous Indian Tribes
George Washington
Hiawatha
King Arthur
Peter Pan
Robert E. Lee
Robin Hood
Robinson Crusoe
Three Little Horses
Three Little Horses at the King's
Palace

Beginner Books

For ages 5-7:
The Cat in the Hat Beginner Book
Dictionary
The Cat in the Hat
The Cat in the Hat Comes Back
Dr. Seuss's ABC Book
Green Eggs and Ham
Go, Dog, Go!
Bennett Cerf's Book of Riddles
The King, the Mice and the Cheese
and other titles

Picture Books

For ages 4 and up:
Poems to Read to the Very Young
Songs to Sing with the Very Young
Stories to Read to the Very Young
Alice in Wonderland
Anderson's Fairy Tales
Bambi's Children
Black Beauty
Favorite Tales for the Very Young
Grandmas and Grandpas
Grimm's Fairy Tales
Heidi
Little Lost Kitten
Mother Goose
Once-Upon-A-Time Storybook
Pinocchio
Puppy Dog Tales
Read-Aloud Nursery Tales
Sleeping Beauty
The Sleepytime Storybook
Stories that Never Grow Old
The Wild and Wooly Animal Book
The Wizard of Oz

RANDOM HOUSE, INC., 457 MADISON AVENUE, NEW YORK 22, N. Y.